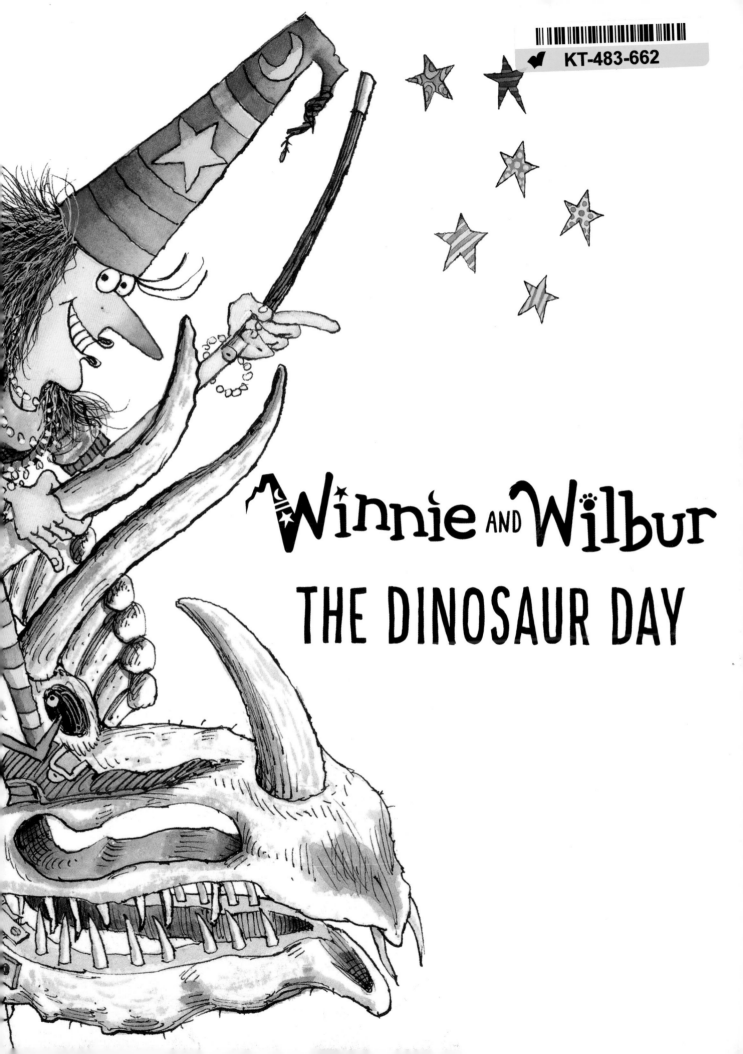

Winnie and Wilbur

THE DINOSAUR DAY

Winnie the Witch and her
big black cat Wilbur loved
to visit the museum.

It was full of fascinating things.

W...bur
SP...LLS

Winn...   DAY

Win...   AY, WINNIE

Win...   KNIGHT

There were bugs and beetles and creepy crawlies and slinky snakes.

There were buttons to push, levers to pull, and games to play.

But best of all was the dinosaur room.
Winnie and Wilbur liked to look at
the bones and footprints and models.

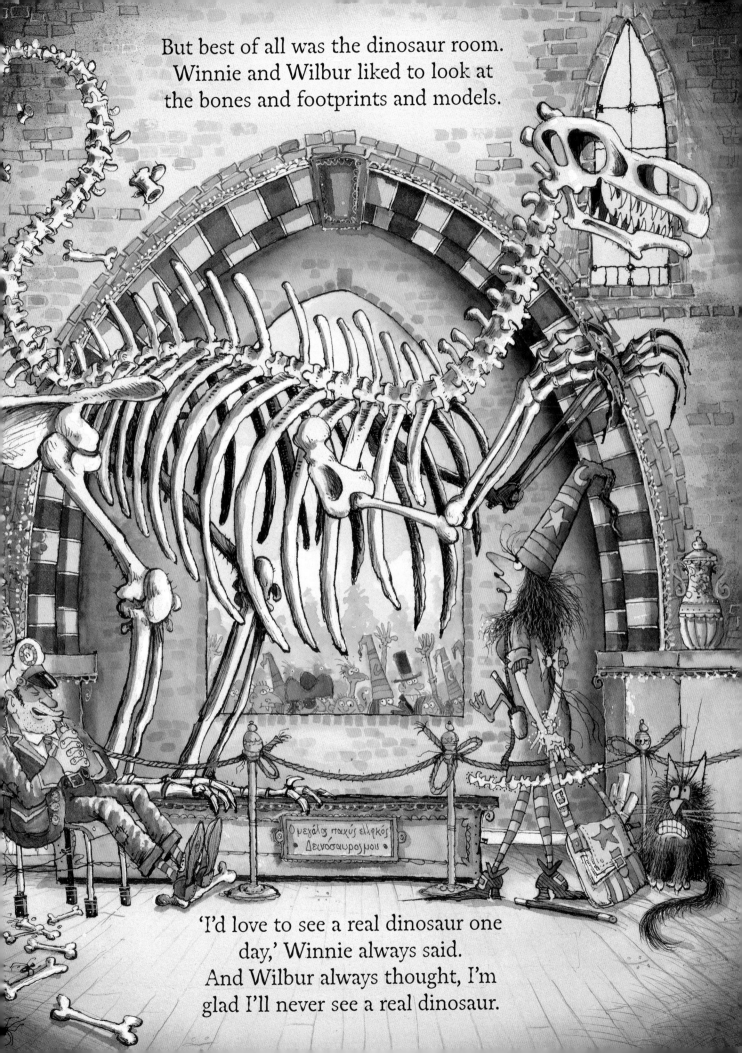

Ο μεγάλος παχύς ελλρκός
Δεινόσαυρος μου

'I'd love to see a real dinosaur one
day,' Winnie always said.
And Wilbur always thought, I'm
glad I'll never see a real dinosaur.

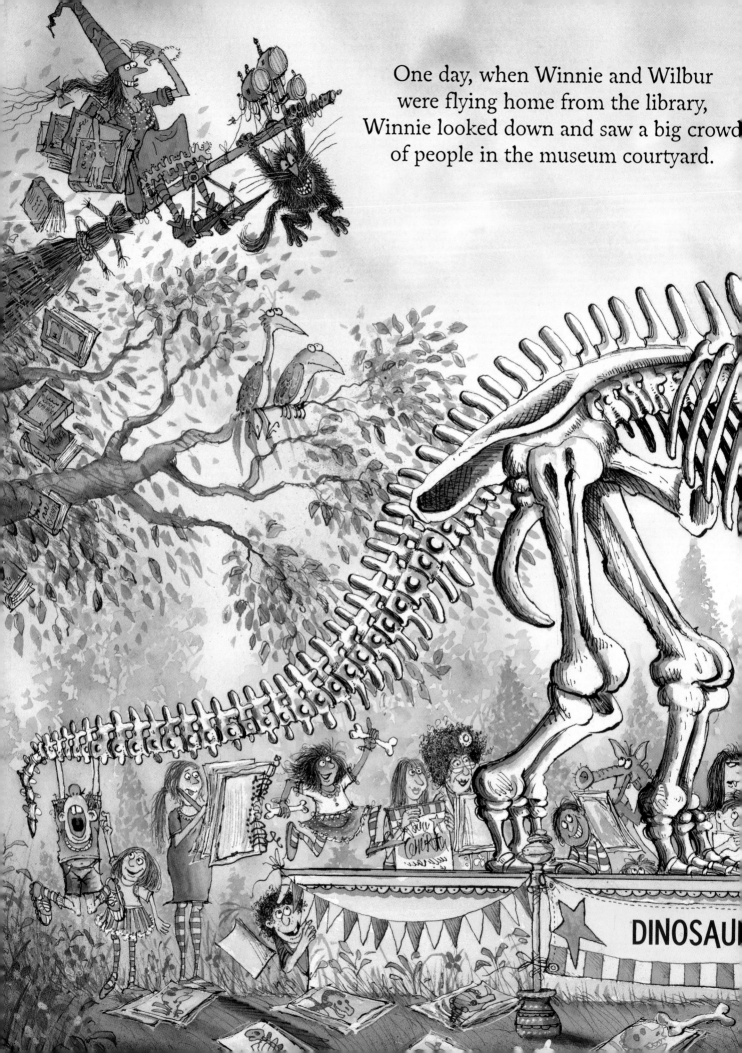

One day, when Winnie and Wilbur
were flying home from the library,
Winnie looked down and saw a big crowd
of people in the museum courtyard.

DINOSAU

'Whatever's happening there?' asked Winnie,
and she flew down to have a look.

There, in the courtyard, was an enormous skeleton.
It was dinosaur week at the museum, and there
was a special competition . . .

WEEK

SPECIAL COMPETITION.
Draw a picture or make a model to show what the **SKELETON** looked like when it was a **DINOSAUR.** AND WIN A PRIZE!

Winnie loved winning prizes.
She looked carefully at the skeleton.
It was very, very big, with lots of spiky bits.

Winnie couldn't decide whether to do a
picture or a model, and she couldn't decide
what the dinosaur might have looked like.

'It's too hard, Wilbur,' Winnie said.
But she really wanted to win the prize.

Then Winnie had an idea.

'Jump on my shoulder, Wilbur,' said Winnie,
and they zoomed up into the sky and back
to Winnie's house.

Winnie got out her
Big Book of Spells.
'Yes!' she said.

She shut her eyes,
stamped her foot
and shouted,

'Abracadabra!'

There was a flash of fire,
a great WHOOOSH . . .

and Winnie and Wilbur were back
in the time of the dinosaurs.

There were dinosaurs everywhere.
Big dinosaurs, enormous dinosaurs,
gigantic dinosaurs!

Winnie and Wilbur hid in a tree.

'Now all we have to do is find a dinosaur
that looks like the skeleton,' said Winnie.
'That should be easy.'
'Meeow,' said Wilbur.
He didn't like the time of the dinosaurs.

Winnie looked around carefully.
'There it is!' she shouted.
'Of course. It's a triceratops.
Look at its three horns, Wilbur.'
'Meeeoow!' said Wilbur.

He didn't want to look.
He wanted to go home.

Winnie got out her drawing book
and her coloured pencils.
It was much easier drawing a *real* dinosaur.

Her drawing looked *exactly* like the triceratops.
Well, it looked quite like the triceratops.

'This is an excellent drawing,' said Winnie.
'It's sure to win the prize.'

But now we need to get back to the museum.
I know! The triceratops can take us.'
'Meeeoow!' said Wilbur.
He put his paws over his eyes.

Winnie picked him up, jumped onto the dinosaur's
back, waved her magic wand and shouted,

'Abracadabra!'

. . . and the dinosaur **WHOOSHED** off to the museum.

Professor Perkins was getting ready to present the prize when the dinosaur landed in the courtyard.

Everybody was very surprised!

'Well,' said Professor Perkins, 'I think we all know who has won the competition.'

And he gave a big shiny medal
to the triceratops.
The dinosaur was delighted.
He had never won a prize before.

Winnie didn't mind too much.

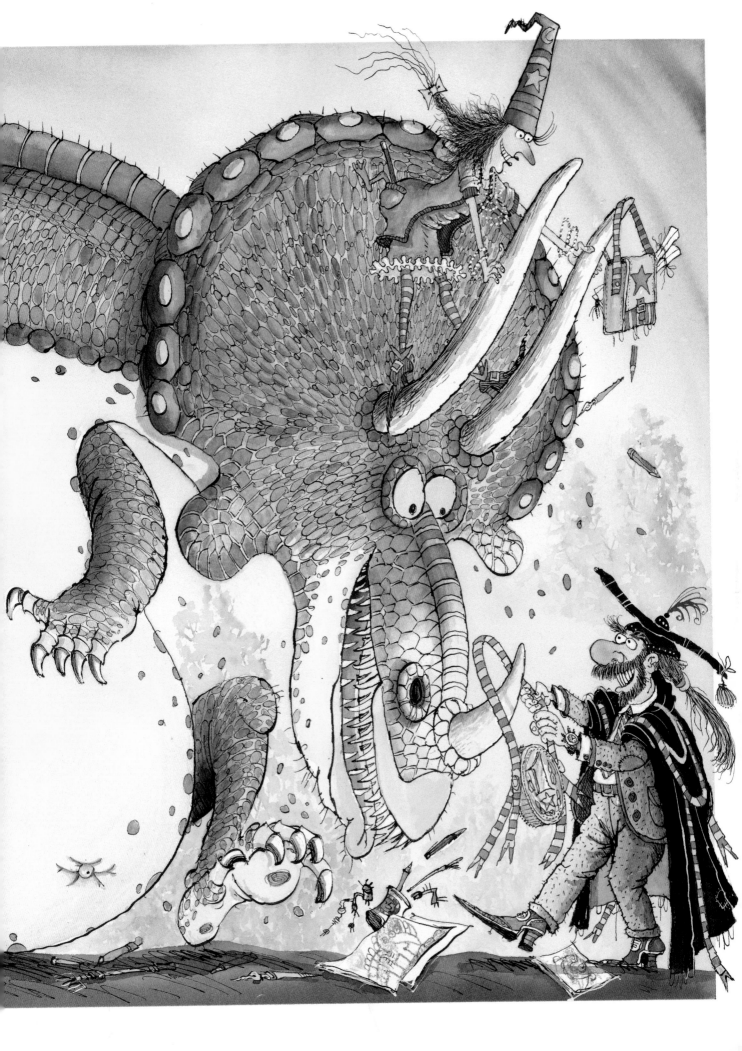

Then Winnie and Wilbur took the
dinosaur home for tea.

The dinosaur didn't like sandwiches
or muffins or cakes.

But he enjoyed eating Winnie's trees
and her roses were delicious.

'Oh dear,' Winnie said. 'He'll eat
my whole garden! It's a pity he's so big,
Wilbur. He's such a nice dinosaur.'

Then Winnie had a wonderful idea.
She waved her magic wand, shouted,

'Abracadabra!'

and the **enormous** dinosaur was a _{tiny} dinosaur.

So now Winnie never has to cut her grass.
And Wilbur has a playmate that is just the right size!

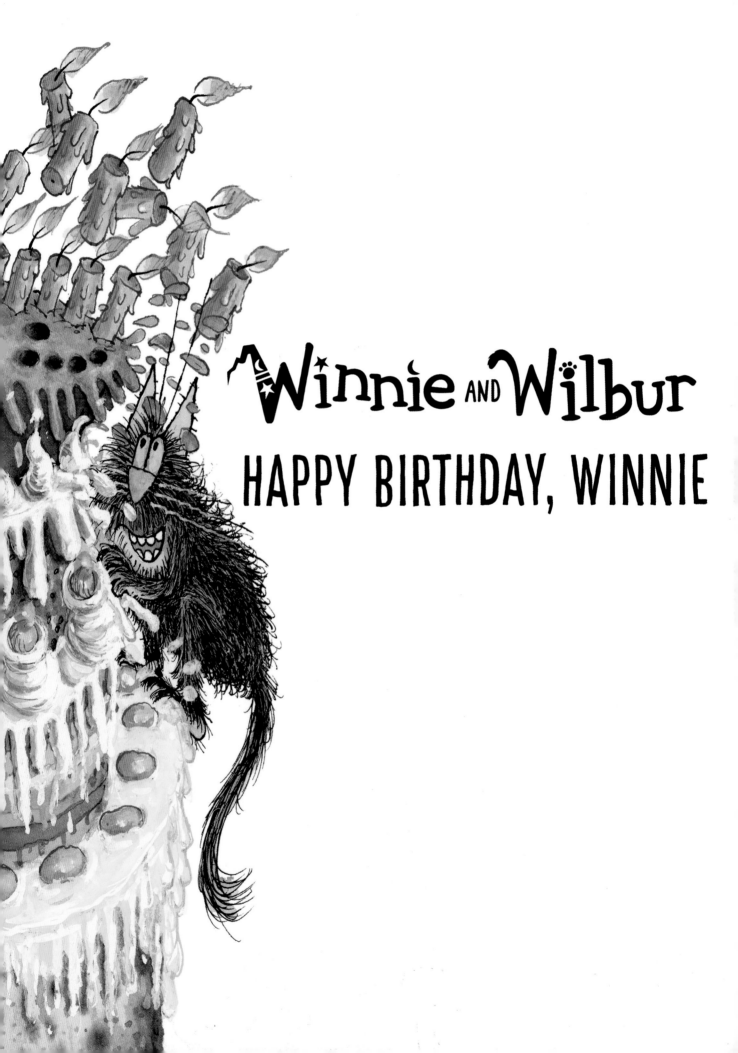

Winnie and Wilbur

HAPPY BIRTHDAY, WINNIE

ΔΕΚΑΤΟΣ ΤΡΙΤΟΣ 1313

FRIDAY
13th.

When Winnie the Witch turned over the
page on her calendar, she saw a big red
circle around Friday the thirteenth.

'That's my birthday!' she said.
'I'll have a party this year, Wilbur.'
'Purr,' said Wilbur. He loved parties.

'What kind of party?' Winnie wondered.
'I know, a garden party.'

On Monday Winnie wrote out the invitations
and sent them by Winni-e-mail.
She invited . . .

Aunty Alice,
Uncle Owen,
her three sisters Wanda, Wilma, and Wendy,
all of her friends,
and Cousin Cuthbert.

On Tuesday she made herself a party dress,
and a matching bow for Wilbur.
'Purr,' said Wilbur. I look lovely, he thought.

On Wednesday Winnie made
lots and lots of food.
Wilbur helped.

WEDNESDAY
11th

Thursday was the day to get the garden ready.
Winnie went outside. It looked rather scruffy.
Then Winnie had a very good idea.
She took out her wand, waved it, shouted,

'Abracadabra!'

. . . and the garden was ready for the party.
'That was easy,' Winnie said.

'Now what else? Oh yes, I need a surprise.
A good party always has a surprise.
I'll have to think about that.'

Friday the thirteenth was a lovely sunny day,
which was lucky.

At two o'clock Winnie's guests arrived.
'Happy birthday, Winnie,' they shouted,
and they piled up the presents on the lawn.

Wanda, Wilma, and Wendy gave Winnie a magic carpet. She'd always wanted one of those.

Uncle Owen gave her a bat in a cage. She'd never wanted one of those.

Aunty Alice gave her a Book of Special Spells,

and there was a magic trumpet from Cousin Cuthbert.

'Let's play some games!' Winnie said.
First they played musical broomsticks.
That was fun, but there was a lot of pushing.
Uncle Owen pushed Aunty Alice into a prickle bush. **Ouch!**

Cousin Cuthbert bounced off a broomstick and landed in the fountain. So they let him win.

'Now we'll have a treasure hunt,' said Winnie.

Uncle Owen looked in the maze, and got lost.

Wilma looked in the bat's cage, and the bat flew away.

Wendy looked in the bouncy castle.
Bang!

Wanda found the treasure, but she had some help.

'The next game is hide-and-seek,' Winnie shouted.
But there was so much noise nobody heard her.

So Winnie picked up her new magic trumpet.
Toot, toot, toot,
Winnie tootled . . .

and **everybody** disappeared.
Winnie was surprised.

Then she was cross.
Where had they gone?

Winnie looked
in the maze.
Nobody.

She looked in the
bat's cage.
Nothing.

She looked in the
bouncy castle.
Nobody.

'Blithering broomsticks!' Winnie said.
'Who will eat all my lovely food?'

Then Winnie saw a label on the trumpet.

IMPORTANT:
to make people disappear, toot three times
to make them come back, stand on your head
and toot three times

So Winnie stood on her head.
Toot, toot, toot,
she tootled . . .

and everybody came back, feeling hungry.
They ate up all the food.

'And now it's time for the surprise,' said Winnie.
She opened her new Book of Special Spells.
'Shut your eyes and think about your
favourite cake!' she said.

Everybody shut their eyes.
Aunty Alice thought about chocolate cake.
Uncle Owen thought about fruit cake.
Cousin Cuthbert thought about rainbow cake.
Wilbur thought about cheesecake.
He loved cheesecake.

Then Winnie the Witch shut her eyes,
turned around three times, stamped her foot,
waved her wand, and shouted,

'Abracadabra!'

. . . and there was the biggest birthday cake
in the whole world,
with candles on the top.

There was a layer of chocolate cake,
a layer of fruit cake,
a layer of rainbow cake,
a layer of cheesecake.
There was strawberry shortcake,
ginger sponge cake,
orange cake,
Black Forest cake.

'How will you blow out the candles?'
asked Cousin Cuthbert.
'That's easy,' Winnie said . . .

and she rode on her magic carpet to the top of the cake.
Puff, puff, puuffffffff!

'Ha ha ha,' laughed Winnie.
'This party is such fun, Wilbur!
I'm a very lucky witch.'

Wilbur didn't say anything.
His mouth was full of cheesecake.
What a lucky black cat!

Happy Birthday to you!

Winnie and Wilbur
THE NAUGHTY KNIGHT

One day, when Winnie the Witch
and her big black cat Wilbur
were flying high over the mountains,
Winnie looked down and saw
an enormous castle.

'Look at that beautiful castle, Wilbur,' Winnie said.
'Let's go and have a look.'

But when they swooped down to the castle
they found it was just a ruin.
'Blithering broomsticks,' said Winnie.
'We are hundreds of years too late.'

Then Winnie had a wonderful idea.
She waved her magic wand, shouted,
'Abracadabra!'

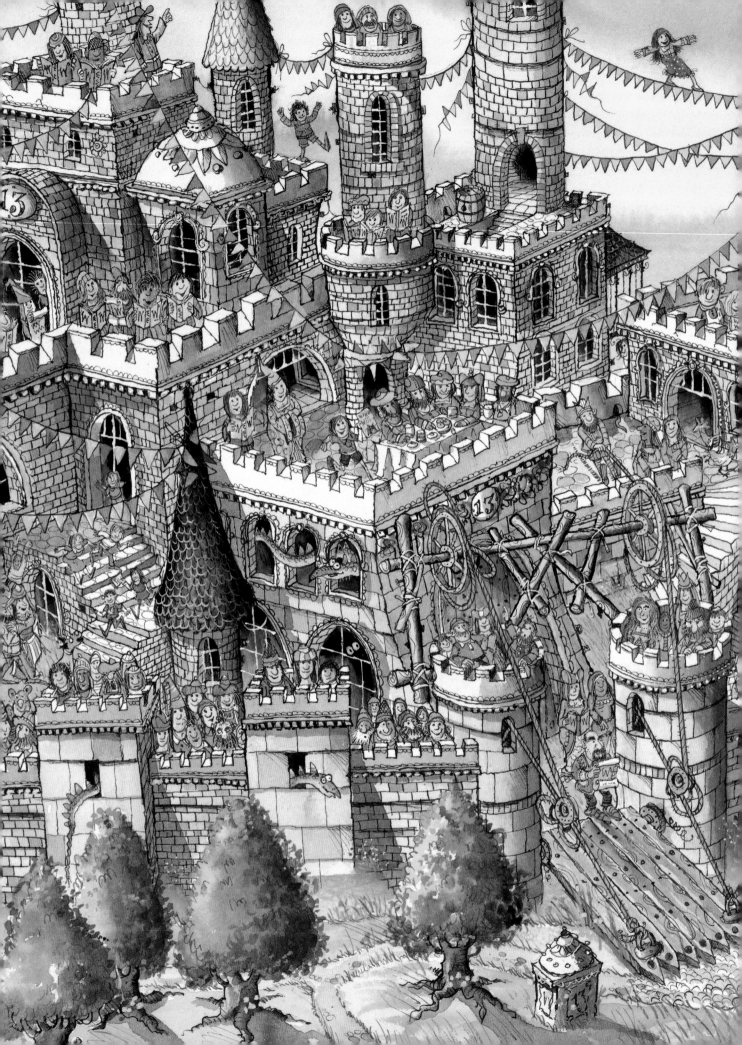

. . . and there was a beautiful castle, just the way it used to be, full of people just the way they used to be.

CRASH! CLANK! CLUNK!

The drawbridge was being lowered over the moat for the king and queen! After them came flags, lovely ladies, and knights in shining armour.

Winnie and Wilbur landed high up in a tower.

'Oooh!' said Winnie. 'Today must
be a special tournament.
We'll go and see what happens.
But first we have to look right.'

Winnie waved her magic wand, shouted,

'Abracadabra!'

and there she was, looking just like the other lovely ladies. Well, she looked a bit like the other lovely ladies.

And Wilbur was a tiny knight in shining armour.

Winnie hid her broomstick, tucked her wand up her sleeve, just in case, and they hurried off to watch the tournament.

The first contest was archery.
There were some very good archers,
but the best was Sir Roderick.
Sir Roderick was huge. He had a big
red face and a big loud voice.

His three arrows all hit the bullseye.
'I am the winner,' he shouted.
'I am the best archer in the kingdom!'

'There is one more archer,' said Winnie.
'Sir Wilbur is an amazing archer.'
'Ha ha ha,' laughed everybody when they
saw Sir Wilbur.
'Ha ha ha ha,' laughed Sir Roderick.

'Abracadabra!'

whispered Winnie,
and she waved her arm.

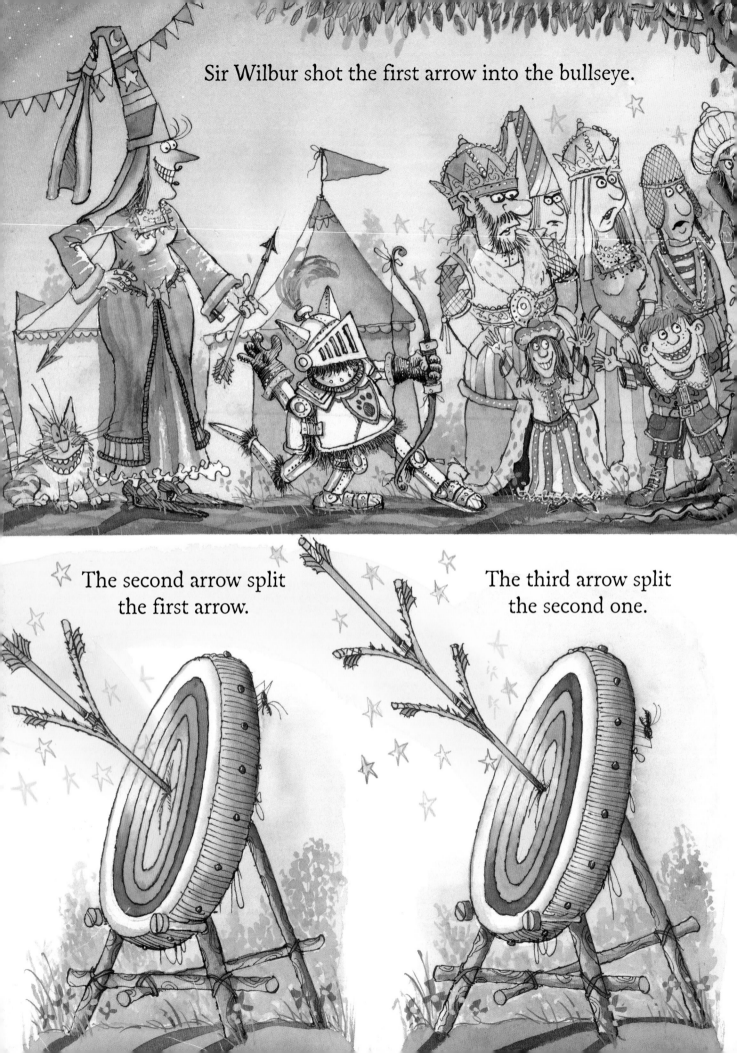

Sir Wilbur shot the first arrow into the bullseye.

The second arrow split
the first arrow.

The third arrow split
the second one.

Amazing! Incredible! Unbelievable!
Sir Wilbur was the winner.

'Grrrr,' snarled Sir Roderick.

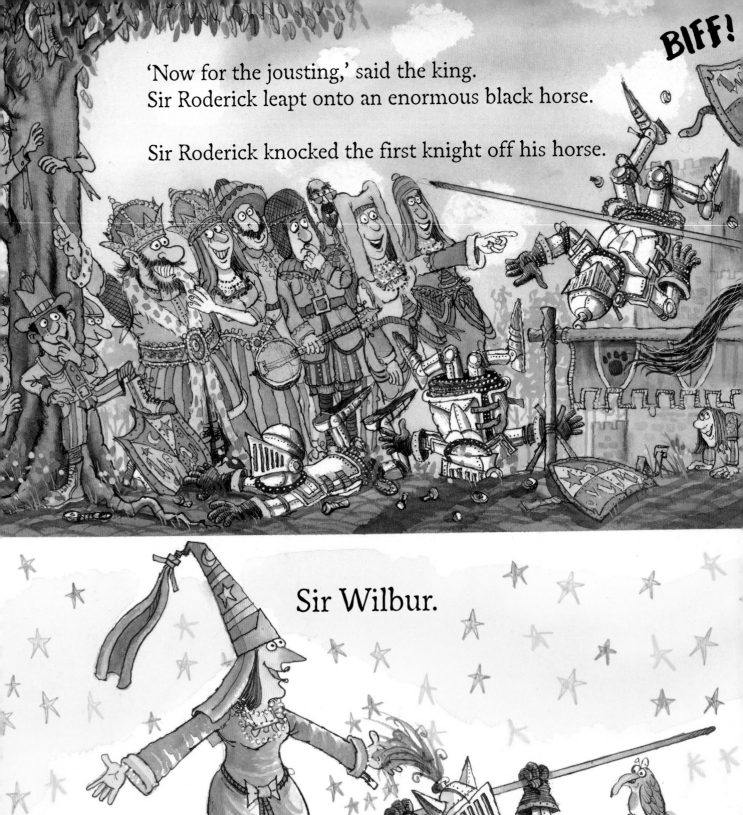

BIFF!

'Now for the jousting,' said the king.
Sir Roderick leapt onto an enormous black horse.

Sir Roderick knocked the first knight off his horse.

Sir Wilbur.

BANG!

Then the second, the third, the fourth, until only one knight was left.

Winnie lifted Sir Wilbur onto an enormous white horse.
'Hold on tight, Wilbur,' she whispered.
'Remember my wand is up my sleeve.'

Into the lists rode Sir Wilbur and Sir Roderick.
They galloped towards each other.
Winnie waved her arm.

'Abracadabra!'

BIFF!

Sir Roderick hit the ground.
Sir Wilbur was the winner.
'Hurrah! Hurrah for Sir Wilbur!'
shouted the crowd.
'Grrrrrr,' snarled Sir Roderick.

BANG!

'It's time for the banquet,' said the king.
'Sir Wilbur will sit next to me.'
'GGGRRRRRR!' snarled Sir Roderick.
He was furious.

He rushed into the Great Hall,
tipped over the soup,
smashed all the pies, and
jumped in the jellies.

What a mess!

She waved her magic sleeve,
whispered,

'Abracadabra!'

and Sir Roderick started to shrink.
He got smaller and smaller . . .

'Hmmm,' said Winnie. 'Sir Roderick needs to be taught a lesson.'

until he was the same size as Sir Wilbur. 'Grrrrrr,' said Sir Roderick.

'Now for the banquet,' Winnie said. She waved her magic sleeve, whispered,

'Abracadabra!'

. . . and there was a magnificent
banquet, even better than the first.

'There is some mighty
magic here today,' said the king.

'Take off your visor, Sir Wilbur.
We want to see your face.'

Oh no!! The king would not be pleased
to see that Sir Wilbur was a cat!

Winnie snatched up Wilbur, raced up the stairs, jumped onto her broomstick, and zoomed up into the sky.

They were soon home again.

'Castles are exciting,' said Winnie.
'But it's lovely to be home again,
isn't it, Wilbur?'

'Purr, purr, purr,' said Wilbur.

OXFORD
UNIVERSITY PRESS

Great Clarendon Street, Oxford OX2 6DP

Oxford University Press is a department of the University of Oxford. It furthers the University's objective of excellence in research, scholarship, and education by publishing worldwide. Oxford is a registered trade mark of Oxford University Press in the UK and in certain other countries

Database right Oxford University Press (maker)

Winnie and Wilbur: The Dinosaur Day first published as Winnie's Dinosaur Day in 2012
Winnie and Wilbur: Happy BIrthday, Winnie first published as Happy Birthday, Winnie in 2007
Winnie and Wilbur: The Naughty Knight first published in 2017
Winnie and Wilbur: Spectacular SPells first published in 2019

The stories are complete and unabridged

British Library Cataloguing in Publication Data available

ISBN: 978-0-19-276888-9

10 9 8 7 6 5 4 3 2 1

Printed in China

Paper used in the production of this book is a natural, recyclable product made from wood grown in sustainable forests. The manufacturing process conforms to the environmental regulations of the country of origin

www.winnieandwilbur.com